Rookie reader

Silly Sally

Written by Betsy Franco
Illustrated by Stacey Lamb

SCHOLASTIC INC.

New York   Toronto   London   Auckland   Sydney
Mexico City   New Delhi   Hong Kong   Buenos Aires

For James
—B.F.

For Charles Schulz
—S.L.

Reading Consultants

Linda Cornwell
Literacy Specialist

Katharine A. Kane
Education Consultant
(Retired, San Diego County Office of Education and San Diego State University)

ISBN 0-516-24159-1

12 11 10 9 8 7 6 5 4 3   7/0

Printed in the U.S.A.   44

First Scholastic printing, October 2002

Sally is so silly!

I smile.

Sally smiles.

I snap.

Sally smiles.

I skip.

Sally smiles.

I sing.

Sally smiles.

Sally smiles.

21

I smile!

Word List (10 words)

I	sing	snap
is	skip	so
Sally	smile	
silly	smiles	

About the Author

Betsy Franco lives in Palo Alto, California, where she has written more than forty books for children—picture books, poetry, and nonfiction. Betsy is the only female in her family, which includes her husband, Douglas, her three sons, James, Thomas, and David, and Lincoln the cat. She starts writing in the wee hours of the morning when everyone but Lincoln is asleep.

About the Illustrator

Stacey Lamb "became" an artist in the fourth grade, when she discovered that she could draw the Peanuts character Snoopy, and has been drawing ever since! She grew up in Illinois and went to the University of Kansas. Today, she lives out in the country in Lawrence, Kansas, with her husband, Brent, two children, Emily and Scott, and one dog, eight cats, one bunny, and one pet mouse.